T0157859

Summer Solstice~ Spirit Horses

Paige Truehart

ISBN: 978-1-4669-3665-2 (sc)
ISBN: 978-1-4669-3664-5 (e)

Trafford rev. 05/17/2012

 www.trafford.com

North America & international
toll-free: 1 888 232 4444 (USA & Canada)
phone: 250 383 6864 ♦ fax: 812 355 4082

Contents

I

Presentation Day

I ROLLED OVER AND SMACKED my blaring alarm clock. It stopped instantly, and I rolled back over and hid under my warm covers. I tried to go back to sleep, but between the sun shining brightly on my face through the window and my Aunt Patty's fist pounding on my door, I couldn't.

"April, it's time to wake up!" Aunt Patty shouted. "You'll be late for school."

I groaned and whipped the covers off of me and rolled out of bed. I had fifteen minutes to get ready and eat breakfast before the bus came.

Aunt Patty couldn't drive me to school since she had to go to work ten minutes earlier then when I go to school.

She owned her own store—Patricia Rose—and made a lot of money, hence the huge mansion I lived in with her.

My parents had died when I was only eight years old. A speeding driver had ran a red light and drove right into my dad's side of the car. Both of my parents were dead instantly. I was still at school, but when I had gotten off the bus at my house, there was a chill in the air. Aunt Patty was waiting for me and she told me the sad news. I had never cried to hard and long in my life. Even worse, the accident was on the news on TV.

I dressed in a simple T-shirt, black leggings, and flats. I braided my dark brown hair down my shoulder and splashed some water into my face after I brushed my teeth.

"I'm leaving!" Aunt Patty called up the sleek wooden stairs.

"Okay, bye," I called back.

I heard the back door close and sped down the stairs, making Aunt Patty's snobby white cat, Pi, hiss and duck under the coffee table in the living room.

I quickly ate a bowl of cereal and was just getting up to wash out the bowl when a voice came from the dining room.

"I'll get that," Jeffery, Aunt Patty's butler, said as he strode into the kitchen.

"I forgot you were still here," I exclaimed. "Aren't you supposed to be at the food market by now?"

Jeffery smiled as he washed out my cereal bowl and spoon. "Not yet. Miss Patty told me to sleep in today. I feel bad about that, but I do what ever she asks."

I stuffed my school bag with books. "That was nice of her. Thanks, Jeffery."

"You're very welcome, Miss April," Jeffery told me as I walked to the front door. "See you after school."

"Bye," I called, shutting the door.

I stepped into the hot June air. One more week of school, then summer. If only today wasn't presentation day in Mr. Lawrence's English class. I wasn't the best speaker on the spot, so I only prayed all would go well and I wouldn't choke up.

We were supposed to read our essay about Shakespeare and give our opinion about his work.

I double-checked that I had my essay paper when the school bus drove up around the curb. I jogged to the doors just as they opened and climbed up the steep stairs.

I glanced around the bus before walking down the skinny aisle. Grace was sitting with her friend, Rachel, and Ricky was sitting with Matt. Then I spotted my friend, Alicia sitting by herself, texting on her phone. She hid it behind the previous seat's back and kept her head down. Laurel, the seventy-year-old bus driver had very strict rules. Number two was no texting. Number one was no standing up.

"Hey," I greeted as I slid into the seat next to Alicia.

"Hi!" she looked up from her purple phone and slid it into her bag. "Ready for English class?"

I moaned. "Nope."

Alicia laughed. "Me either."

"Do you at least have your paper?"

"Yes," she said, sighing. "I just texted Sasha to grab her paper before she leaves her house."

"Good," I said. "She always forgets everything."

"I know," Alicia said. She leaned back onto the head rest and closed her eyes. Faint gray marks were under her eyes and her usually tan skin was a little pale.

"You okay?" I asked gently.

She barely nodded.

"Something wrong?"

"No," Alicia replied quietly. "I've just been up with these stupid nightmares."

"What kind of nightmares?" I asked

"The kinds that keep you up all night," Alicia said, a hint of tease in her voice.

"Well, yeah, but I meant what happened," I told her.

"Oh." Alicia wrinkled her nose and small creases appeared on her forehead. That's what she did when she was thinking. "Well, some kind of dark figure is chasing me through the woods. And I can't get away." She paused. "These bright orange lights flash everywhere and then they change to blue. Then to white. Then to gray. And just before the figure grabs me, I wake up."

I listened carefully. "Wow. That's weird."

Alicia nodded. "I've had them three nights in a row."

"Have you told anybody? Maybe you need to go to a therapist or something," I said.

Alicia opens her eyes and looks at me. "No," she said. "I didn't think it was that bad."

I shrugged and sat back with her. I had nightmares a lot when my parents died. But they stopped after a couple of months. They weren't anything like what Alicia had described.

Finally, the bus turned a corner and Sacramento High was in view. Students trampled each other to get inside, while some just sat on the stone benches near the entrance and just talked or texted on phones.

Alicia and I waited until the other people stepped off the bus and then we got up.

Just as we were opening the doors to the school, somebody called our names.

I turned to see Sasha running over to us. Her sandy hair was in a bun, but half of it had fallen out. She was in sweat pants too big for her and a saggy sweatshirt. She almost tripped on her pant leg while she ran.

"Hey, guys," she greeted.

"What's wrong with you?" Alicia asked, raising her thin light brown eyebrows.

Sasha sighed and felt her hair. "Aw, man! I fixed my hair twice this morning!"

"No sleep?" I asked.

"No," replied Sasha, taking her hair down. She fluffed it with her hand and threw it into another messy bun.

"Same," Alicia said.

"Really? What happened?" Sasha asked.

"Nightmares," Alicia said. She told Sasha what had happened in her dreams.

"I couldn't sleep because my parents were up all night, fighting."

I couldn't help but feel bad for Sasha. Her parents always fought with each other and didn't care if Sasha—and her friends, if she had some over—saw them.

"So," I said, trying to change the subject. "You have your essay, right?"

"Mmm-hmm," Sasha nodded, pulling out the paper.

"Good, Mr. Lawrence said you'll get a zero if it's late," Alicia said.

We walked down the main hall and separated to go to our lockers. I opened mine and traded my math book for my English book since I had math in the afternoon. The first bell rang, and I rushed into Ms. Waller's classroom. Once the second bell rang and you weren't in her classroom in your seat, she considered you late.

Ms. Waller was an old, old lady. Her snowy white hair was a thin cloud on her pale head and permanent wrinkles showed on her forehead. Her cracked lips were turned down at the corners and purple circles were always under her eyes. Today she wore another one of her crazy outfits—bright orange skinny jeans *(ouch)*, a pale pink T-shirt that said TEACHER FOR SALE (okay???), and blue clogs.

I tried not to stare as I walked in and slid into my assigned seat next to Logan Rydell and Whitney Holms.

Whitney tapped on my desk with her pencil.

"Hey," I said, turning to her. We had five minutes before the second bell rang.

"Do you have the homework?" she said in a hurried whisper.

I nodded. "Why? Do you need it?" I started turning to get my homework out of my bag. It wasn't too hard, but Whitney also wasn't the brightest kid in class. I retrieved the sheet of paper and handed it to Whitney.

"Thank you! I asked Jamie but she didn't do it either," Whitney replied.

"Well, lucky I came in," I joked, trying to smile.

I always seemed to be the go-to person when someone needed homework or anything else related to school—

pencils, pens, paper, highlighters, work. If I did the work and got my own supplies, why can't they, too? It's not that hard!

I sat in my seat next to Alicia in English and took a deep breath. Presentation day. Why did Mr. Lawrence have to hate me so much? It turned out that he had picked me to go first, and I slowly made my way up to the front of the classroom.

I almost tripped over Rudy Baker's chair and that made the whole class laugh. Great. They're already warmed up.

I swallowed hard and stood by Mr. Lawrence. He wore a plaid button-down and tan pants. His gray hair only grew around the ears, bottom of his head, leaving a large bald spot on the top. His beard was connected to his mustache and had the same gray color as his head hair but was mixed with some white. And, to top it all off, he had a huge zit on the end of his nose that he never bothered to take care of. Gross.

I rubbed my nose, trying to keep the smell of Mr. Lawrence away from me. He smelled of too much cologne and wet dog. I could barely stand it. I inched away from him and started reading.

I stammered a little and had to repeat things a few times because someone always claimed they couldn't hear me, but I finally finished.

"Now, what do you think of Shakespeare, Miss Cincinnati?" Mr. Lawrence asked, his crooked yellow teeth in my face. I jerked my head back slightly and gave him a tight smile.

"I think Shakespear is amazing. The way he writes is wonderful and is full of . . . of . . . . emotion," I spit out. I didn't realize I hadn't thought that part over until now.

"Good," Mr. Lawrence said, nodding.

I prayed he didn't ask any other questions. I had nothing.

"Okay, up next is . . ." Mr. Lawrence scanned his list.

I practically sprinted to my desk and, again, almost tripped over Rudy's chair that stuck out in the aisle.

"I'm going to kill him," I mutter under my breath as the class burst out laughing. Anything will get them laughing.

"Come on up, Leigh-Ann," Mr. Lawrence called.

Leigh-Ann, a petite girl with short brown hair walked up to the front and began. I envied her confidence, from the way she walked up to the front down to the way she took a tiny bow at the end.

"Thank you, Leigh-Ann," Mr. Lawrence said, waving her back to the rows of desks. "Stephen? Are you ready?"

I tuned out the other presentations for the rest of class. Most of the students got theirs in, but some had to wait until tomorrow.

"Alright, class," Mr. Lawrence said. "See you tomorrow."

We all gathered our books and papers and fled.

I walked into the cafe and got in the lunch line. Even though I didn't eat lunch since the food was so disgusting, I still made it look like I was getting food into my system. I mean, it wasn't like I was starving myself. I practically ate the whole kitchen when I got home!

I gathered some food and a carton of milk, paid the lunch lady, and scanned the cafe for Sasha and Alicia. I spotted them at our usual table. They were both picking at their food, too. I could see their disgusted faces from where I stood.

I let my tray clatter down onto the table and sat down next to Sasha.

"How was English?" Sasha asked. She had English after lunch.

"Fine," I said, playing with the gross-looking slab of meat on my plate.

"It wasn't as bad as you thought, right?" Sasha asked.

I shook my head. Then shrugged. "I don't know."

"A girl of very few words today, huh?" Alicia said.

I shrugged again. I didn't really know what to say.

"So, after school tomorrow I say we go to the beach," Alicia said. "I just bought a new bathing suit and I'm dying to wear it."

"Okay," Sasha agreed. "April?"

I nodded. "Yeah, sure."

"I'll drive," Alicia said.

II

Beach

THE SUN LOOKED PROMISING ON Friday and I was getting excited. It was around one thirty and I was sitting in math class, copying down Mrs. Richard's math notes.

"Alright class," Mrs. Richard said, capping her dry-erase marker. "Since I'm the best teacher ever, I'm going to let you out five minutes early. But for right now, you guys can just visit with each other quietly."

A collective "yes!" went through the room and Mrs. Richard chuckled and began typing on her computer.

Neither Sasha or Alicia were in my math class, but Jenna Quaker was. We used to live next to each other before I moved in with Aunt Patty. I still remember Mrs. Quaker telling me how Jenna and I used to play in Jenna's kiddy pool all the time in the summer.

I turned my chair toward Jenna and hers was already facing me. We laughed.

"So, got anything planned this weekend?" Jenna asked me.

I nodded. "Beach with Sasha and Alicia."

"Fun," Jenna said. "I'm going to the movies with Katie."

"What movie are you seeing?" I asked.

"Oh, we still have to decide," Jenna replied. "But it's definitely between that romantic comedy and the new scary one."

"Cool," I said. "I'm sure they'll both be great."

"So, what's going on with you?" Jenna asked. "I feel like we haven't talked in forever." When she laughs, she sounds tired. And that's when I notice the faint gray circles under her eyes.

Ignoring her question, I said, "Have you been up all night?" I couldn't hold it in. Right after the words came out, I slapped my hand over my mouth. "Sorry."

Jenna smiled and shakes her head. "It's fine. And yeah, I couldn't get much sleep. I've been having these nightmares about the weirdest things!"

"What happened in them?" I asked.

Jenna told me exactly what Alicia had. I sit back in my chair when she's finished and think. "That's weird," I say finally.

"It is?" Jenna asked.

"Well, Alicia told me the exact same thing," I told her. "She has nightmares, too."

"Hmm," Jenna said. "That *is* weird."

"Yeah," I said. "But I'm sure it's just a coincidence."

Jenna nods. "Probably."

But was it just a coincidence?

After school, I met Alicia and Sasha by Alicia's dad's blue truck. It was huge. Like, when I tried to get in I literally had to hop into the vehicle.

"Pretty cool, huh?" Alicia grinned as she strapped on her buckle.

"It's enormous!" Sasha exclaimed. She sat in the back with all the beach stuff while I sat in the front with Alicia. Sasha had this never-dying fear that if we got in an accident and she was sitting in the front, she would get suffocated by the air bag.

"I know," Alicia replied. "My dad said it was the most expensive car he bought."

"That's no surprise," I said.

It took about an hour to get to the beach. We talked and joked all the way there, and time flew by. It surprised me when I heard laughing and girly screams. I looked up and saw a father run to his daughter, picked her up, and swung her around in a circle. The girl, who looked like around eight, screeched and laughed. I couldn't help feeling sorry for myself that that kind of thing couldn't happen to me anymore. Not just because I was sixteen now, but because my parents were dead.

"Come on, let's go!" Alicia said after she parked the truck. It took up two whole parking spaces.

We unloaded the truck and walked along the boardwalk, our arms full. We passed numerous stores along the way. T-shirt stores, a tattoo shop where a woman was getting a tattoo on her ankle, fried dough and lemonade shops, and beachy jewelry stores.

Sasha pointed to the beach where all you could see were rainbow-colored umbrellas. But she was pointing to a small, unoccupied space that would be perfect. We crossed the boardwalk and stepped down onto the burning hot sand. I took off my flip-flops and carried them to avoid flipping dirt into people's faces and onto their blankets or towels. Alicia and Sasha did the same.

We set down our things and while Sasha set up the umbrella and Alicia fanned out the towels and laid them next to each other, I sorted out the snacks like a tiny buffet.

We slathered on sun screen and laid out on our towels after taking off our cover-ups. My already-tan skin didn't burn that easily—usually I didn't get burned at all and just got more tan. But now I would have tan lines because of the bathing suit. Oh well.

After about an hour of lying in the sun, I thought my skin was about to burn off.

"I'm going to go cool down," I said to Alicia and Sasha. "Be right back."

"Alright," Alicia said, her eyes still closed. "When you come back we should get ice cream or something."

"Okay," I said, wiping sand off my burning legs.

I got up and swerved around lots of people lying in the sun. After getting out of the jungle of people, I walked all the way down the beach to the end where a mountain of rocks were. Beyond them was a patch of green trees. A little boy picked up a small rock and gasped.

"Mommy, mommy!" he cried. "Look what I found!"

His mother walked over to him and bent down. But soon after she screeched and jumped back, almost loosing her straw hat. The little boy was dangling a bright red crab in front of his mother's face.

"Daniel! Put that thing down!" the mother shouted.

"Bye, crabby," Daniel said and he replaced the rock after setting the crab back down. I grinned as the mother stomped off while the little boy hid his smile.

I stepped into a cool patch of water where nobody was and let myself float in the icy water. It soothed my burning skin but soon after it began to give me freezer burn since I wasn't moving. I got out.

Just as I was about to walk back to Alicia and Sasha, I thought of something. Wouldn't it be hilarious to pull what that little boy did? Sasha was the perfect victim.

I staggered along the rocks until I found the one the little boy picked up. Sure enough, the little crab was in a tiny pool of water along with some snails.

I leaned in to pick it up, but stopped when I heard a sound coming from the trees. I looked up, expecting more little kids, but no one was there. Without thinking I dropped the rock and began wandering over to the patch of forest. I made sure I was quiet so I wouldn't scare off whatever was in there.

Finally I hopped off the last rock and walked over soft, brown grass mixed with thick, dark brown dirt. I peeked into the woods, holding onto a strong tree trunk. The bark scratched at my hands, but I didn't care.

I heard the sound again. It was a rustling. It sounded like something was in a bush about ten feet away from me.

"Hello?" I whispered. "Who's there?"

Nothing.

The sound came again.

"It someone there?" I called quietly.

Nothing answered, so I moved forward a bit. Curiosity took over. For all I knew, a killer with a chain saw could be in that bush. But my feet kept moving my body closer and closer.

Just when I was about five feet away a figure jumped out of the bush and ran. I squinted and tried to figure out what it was. It was brown and white. It was long legs, and it was fast. It was big. But how could it have hid behind that tiny bush? I shrugged to myself and began to look on the ground for any footprints. Or paw prints. Whatever that thing was, it didn't leave anything.

I made my way back to Sasha and Alicia, forgetting all about the trick I wanted to play. But I didn't care; all I could think off was that huge creature. I didn't say a thing to Alicia and Sasha. It just seemed too complicated. But I would tell them sooner or later. Right after I found out what that thing was.

III

Earth

THAT NIGHT I COULDN'T SLEEP. My mind was still on that mysterious creature. But finally, when I fell asleep and woke up to a bright, sunny day, I knew where I wanted to go.

At breakfast, Jeffery set a plate of eggs, bacon, toast, home fries, and sausage in front of me. There was always a huge plate in front of me for meals but I only ate half of it every time.

Aunt Patty sipped her coffee and quietly read the paper across from me.

"Aunt Patty?"

"Yes, April?"

"I'm going back to the beach," I said.

"Again? Why?" Aunt Patty questioned.

"It was so fun yesterday," I stammered, "and, um, Alicia and Sasha wanted to go again . . . today."

"Alright," Aunt Patty said. "But don't get too much sun. You're already crazy," she added with a smirk.

"Ha ha," I said, standing up. Just as I was about to clear my plate, Jeffery stole it from me.

"I'll clean this up, Miss April," Jeffery said. "You go have fun."

I thanked him and went upstairs. I dressed in shorts, a tank top, and flip flops. I took a bag with me so Aunt Patty wouldn't question where all my towels and sun blocks were.

"Can I borrow your convertible today?" I asked Aunt Patty when I went back downstairs.

"*You* want to drive?" Aunt Patty asked, raising her eyebrows.

I had a bad fear of driving ever since my parents died. I just didn't want that same thing to happen to me.

I gulped. "Yeah, why not? Alicia drove yesterday, so its only fair that I drive today."

Aunt Patty looked at me. "Okay," she said very slowly. "Here." She handed me her keys.

"Thanks, love you," I called as I shut the door.

I felt bad for lying to Aunt Patty, but I had no choice. There was no way I could lie to my friends, too, and then just go off into the woods while they're burning in the sun waiting for me to get back.

I drove to the beach. It took twice the time just because I was going so slow. I was surprised a police officer didn't give me a ticket for going so slow.

I finally parked the car in a space by the boardwalk and hopped out.

I cut across the beach and went straight to the woods. There wasn't anybody near the rocks today, thank goodness. That would be awkward if I was looking in the woods for some creature while they're watching me like I'm crazy.

Maybe I am crazy.

Aunt Patty said I was, but that was only a joke.

I climbed over the sharp rocks and stood by the same tree as yesterday, listening for any sounds.

And then it came.

The sound.

The rustling.

From the same bush.

And this time, it didn't run. The creature stepped out in the open where I could see it clearly. It was a large brown and white horse.

I gasped and jumped back, but then calmed myself down. It was only a horse. But was it wild? Dangerous?

I slowly moved towards it, again my curiosity winning over my safety.

The horse was three times the size of any normal sized horse. My head was equal to the knee. Other then its size the horse looked normal. Brown eyes. Soft hair. Hooves. But then I looked up at the mane and tail.

Instead of hair, floating dirt grew from the neck. I stood on a nearby rock and ran my hand through the mane. My hand came out brown with dirt.

"What is this?" I said to myself.

The animal turned its head to me. Its head was the size of half of my body. Its eyes as big as basketballs. But they had some sort of gentleness to them. A kindness that only my mother had in her eyes.

I was mesmerized.

I stroked the creature's long nose. The muzzle was velvet soft and pink like cotton candy. But the next thing that happened took me off guard and I almost fell off the rock.

"April," the horse spoke.

"You-you . . ." I couldn't get it out. "You just talked?" My mind went blank and my head spun around like a Ferris wheel.

"April, you have to calm down," the horse said. "I need you to know something."

I still couldn't process that a horse was talking. I never believed in those stupid stories that had talking animals. But? What is this?

All of a sudden, the whole world seemed to stop. I tilt my head to the side, my eyes squinting and focused on the horse's face.

Something familiar about someone . . .

"Mom?"

The horse—believe it or not—smiled. "Yes, April."

"What the heck?" I said to myself, smacking my forehead. "What is going on?" I stepped off the rock and paced back and forth.

"April, I'm not "mom" anymore," the horse said.

"What? Of course you are! That is your voice! I know it!" I shouted.

"April, calm down," the horse said, taking a step toward me. "I'm your mother, yes, in a Spirit Horse's body. But you can not call me mom. This Spirit Horse's body's name is Earth. I am now Earth to you."

"Earth? Spirit Horse?" I almost passed out. "What's that?"

"When someone dies," the horse—Earth—said, "their body gets transferred into a Spirit Horse's body if they are supposed to go to heaven. You don't choose this. They do."

"Who?"

"All of the Gods," Earth said. "We are transferred into Spirit Horse's bodies so we can help the planet. There are many of us. I am Earth, your—"

"Dad? He's here too?" I asked.

"Yes, April," Earth said. "He's here. He is Fire."

"Fire," I whispered. "How does that help?"

"In many ways," Earth said. "Let me explain. Spirit Horses each have their own distinct look. They have their own power. I'm brown and white, with a dirt mane and tail. I'm Earth. I can stop earthquakes if I can feel them. Fire is a chestnut horse and his mane and tail are flames. He can stop fires when he smells them. Water is a gray horse with flows of water for a mane and tail—she can stop hurricanes and tsunamis. Snow is a white horse with a snowy mane and tail. She can stop avalanches when she feels the cold on her back. And last in our heard, Storm, is a black horse with a windy mane and tail. He stops tornadoes and lightning. You see, we are all very special in one way. And the planet needs us."

"Wow," I said. "That's amazing!"

"But remember April," Earth warned me. "You can not tell our secret to anyone."

"Why?"

"Because people will take the planet for granted. They will not worry about deaths or disasters."

"What's so bad about that?" I asked.

"It will over-populate. Without these natural disasters, people would be everywhere and things, like pollution and what not, would just get worse. The job of the Spirit Horse is to let people survive. But you need to earn it. We can't stop every single disaster. But we try."

"Oh" is all I can say.

"Don't worry, April," Earth said. "I know you. You can keep a secret. We trust you."

"You can trust me," I said. "Where are the others?"

"In our meadow," Earth said. "Would you like to meet them?"

"Okay," I said. I wanted to hear my father's voice again.

"Don't touch any of them, though," Earth said. "Unless you want to get burned, wet, freezing, or shocked. If you touch me, you'll just get plain dirty."

"Wow," I said. "Thanks for the heads-up."

"Of course," Earth said. "Here we go."

"Can I ride on your back?"

"If you don't mind getting your bottom dirty," Earth said.

"I don't care," I said.

"Alright then, hop on," Earth said. She lowered herself to her knees, like a camel, and I climbed on. Right away, I felt the dirt in her mane. But I clung on to it because she was so tall, I didn't want to fall off.

"Hold on," Earth said.

I braced myself.

Earth galloped through the trees, weaving them in and out. Three times taller then a normal horse, three times faster. My hair blew back and I didn't even want to know what my face looked like. Finally, Earth slowed and she knelt down. I got off.

"Ready?" she asked.

I nodded.

IV

Meeting the Herd

T HE MEADOW WAS A BRIGHT place. The leaves on the trees that surrounded the large area were all the perfect shade of emerald. The trees' bark was a deep shade of brown. The meadow grass—shortened from the grazing of the Spirit Horses—was a light green. The sky above was a clear, light blue and exactly two clouds, white and fluffy, were on either side of the meadow. A patch of wild flowers— purples, pinks, yellows, and oranges—was on the west side of the meadow. Right in the middle were the horses. All the same size. All different colors.

"Come along," Earth said, nudging me.

I hadn't noticed I had stopped. "Oops, sorry."

"It's fine, April," Earth said. "Come on."

We walked over to the horses.

The first to come over to us was a dapple gray horse. I was guessing that was Water by the flows of water coming from her neck and rump.

"Hello," she said. Her voice also sounded familiar . . .

"Nana?" I asked, my mouth widening.

"Yes, but now I am Water," the horse said.

"Of course, of course," I said. "Sorry."

"It's quite all right, April," Water said, smiling. "Wow, do you look big!"

"Water," Earth said sternly.

"Sorry, Earth," Water said. "I couldn't help it."

Next Storm came over. He sounded like Grandpa. But I held that in.

"Hello, young one," Storm said. He was gorgeous—coal black. His mane and tail looked like hair, but they constantly blew around as if wind were going though them.

"Hi," I said.

Next came Fire. Dad.

"April," Fire said. "I've missed you."

"You too," I said. I wish I could hug him, but I didn't want to risk getting a burn. Fire looked the scariest—chestnut hair with flames growing from his neck, between his ears, and out behind him. He also had feathers—the hair that grew on a draft horse's leg about half way down—and they were flames, too.

The last horse didn't come over.

"Snow," Earth called. "Come over."

Snow was lying down, but she didn't look up.

"Snow's a little . . ." Earth couldn't think of the right word.

"Snobby," Storm did it for her.

"I guess," Earth said.

Snow finally came over.

"Why would I want to meet *her?*" Snow said. "She's the reason I'm here!"

I got very confused. But then . . . oh. She was absolutely right.

I *was* the reason why she was now a Spirit Horse. Cousin Jillian. When we were both twelve, we were going to a birthday party. Aunt Patty's car had one seat left and I had made Jillian go in the car with Mr. Walker so I could be with all my friends. We had fought over this, but I finally won by getting the last seat and buckling up. Jillian had to go with Mr. Walker. But they had gotten in a car accident. Both died. And the last thing I remembered was sticking my tongue out at Jillian.

"I am so sorry about that, Jillian," I said. "I mean Snow."

"Whatever, April," Snow said. "If you didn't make me go in there, I wouldn't be *here.*"

"I'm sorry!" I said. I felt horrible.

"You should be," Snow snapped.

"Hey!" Earth shouted. "Snow, calm down. You don't have any reason to snap at her like that. It wasn't her fault Mr. Walker couldn't drive."

Snow opened her mouth, but didn't say anything. I apologized again.

"There's no need to apologize, April," Earth told me. "Snow is just stuck in the past."

Snow snorted and stuck her chin high in the air.

"So, what exactly do you do?" I asked.

"Well, we keep the world at peace," Fire said. "We stop what causes deaths."

"But only if those certain people earn it," Storm added.

"So how do your powers work? Like, how do you know when someone's in trouble?" I asked.

"Vibrations," Water said.

"Whenever something that we can stop is going to happen, we can feel it in our bones," Storm said.

"When did these herds start?"

"When Fire and I died," Earth replied. "For some reason this family is destined to make a difference in the world, and now we are doing it."

"So only the Cincinnati family can become Spirit Horses?" I said.

"So far," Fire said. "We don't know if other people that have crossed over can join us yet."

"Will I join you guys?" I asked.

"Possibly," Water said. "But not for a very long time. Hopefully."

I nodded in understanding. You never knew what could happen in life. And you couldn't stop it, either. Even if you wanted to. Death got what it wanted.

"You said there are other herds," I said, turning to Earth. "Where are they?"

"They're all in different countries. The Dobbin family takes care of Canada. The Clerks take care of Mexico," Earth responded.

"Oh," I said. "So you guys take care of the United States?"

All of them nodded but Snow, who was still ignoring me.

"Uh oh," Storm said.

"What is it, Storm?" Fire asked.

Storm seemed to vibrate then stood tall. "A tornado is on its way to Dallas, Texas."

Earth gave him one nod, and Storm was off. His legs were just a black blur as he galloped off into the trees.

"How long will it take him to get there?" I asked.

"Not long," Water said. "He'll be back before nightfall."

"There's night here?" I asked.

Earth chuckled. "Of course. We need our sleep, too. But we take several naps instead of sleeping for the whole night."

Suddenly Snow jumped to her feet and shook her mane, sending snowflakes everywhere. They reached my skin but melted right away.

"What's wrong?" Fire asked her.

Snow stepped up to me. "She's staying for the night?" Her voice was filled with hate.

"No, no," I said in a rush. "I have to be going soon."

"Great," Snow said, tossing her head. She began grazing by the wildflowers.

I watched her, but quickly turned my head in fear of getting her angry again.

"Don't worry about Snow there, April," Fire whispered. "She's been having a bad day."

"Yeah," Water added. "Just ignore her."

I looked at each of them and saw in their eyes that they really cared. They were family. Nana and Grandpa, Mom and Dad, Jillian. Of course they cared. They were still themselves but in horse-form. Big horse-form.

"We also have our own colors and flowers," Earth said, trying to change the subject.

"Really?" I asked. "What are they?"

Earth's color is lavender and her flower is an Iris.

Fire's color is dark orange and his flower is the buttercup.

Water's color is pale blue and her flower the lily.

Storm's color is navy blue and his flower is the Black Eyed Susan.

And Snow's color is baby pink and her flower is the tulip.

The horses only ate the meadow's grass and drank the water from the stream in the same place. Animals never bothered them and they never bothered other animals. Sometimes they would have a quick chat with a chipmunk or something. After a while, I checked my phone clock. It had been four hours since I told Aunt Patty about going to the beach again.

"I've got to go," I said.

"Already?" Water asked.

Storm had come back while Earth was telling me about the stream. He had saved the whole town from the tornado that he said was one of the biggest he's ever seen.

"Yeah, Aunt Patty is probably expecting me soon," I said. "It was nice seeing you all. I miss you so much."

"You too, April," Fire said. He nodded to me.

I said goodbye to all of them then went on my way. It was probably around one and the beach was fuller then ever. People roamed the shore, kids searched for creatures under the rocks, daredevils swam deep into the ocean, and lots of umbrellas sat in the sand.

I weaved around a little girl carrying a bucket of snails and walked across the beach, across the boardwalk, and down to Aunt Patty's car.

It took a while, but I finally got home.

V

Something New

THE DAYS PASSED BY AND SOON the last day of
school came. June twelfth.

At lunch, I thought about sharing the Spirit Horses with
Sasha and Alicia. But when I opened my mouth to talk,
nothing came out. Then I remembered.

Remember April, you can not tell our secret to anyone.

Why?

Because the people will take the world for granted.

Oh.

So I closed my mouth and stood up to throw away
my tray. Sasha and Alicia followed my lead, but didn't say
anything.

"I'm so happy it's the last day," Sasha said as we sat back
down. "Just two more classes till summer!"

"I know," I said. "I'm excited too."

"I'm having a huge pool party on the twentieth. Almost the whole tenth grade is invited. You guys are coming, right?" Alicia said.

"Of course," I said. "Why the twentieth?"

"We're getting a new liner in so it won't be ready until then," Alicia answered.

"Oh," I said. "Well that's a good reason."

Finally, school ended and we cleaned out our lockers, returned our books, and said goodbye to our classmates and teachers. The final bell rang and Sasha, Alicia and I stepped out of the stuffy school and out into the fresh, warm air.

At home, Jeffery was cleaning the kitchen counter with a sponge. He smiled and waved when he saw me.

"Hello, Miss April," Jeffery said. "How was the last day?"

"Fine," I said, shrugging my school bag off my sore shoulders.

"Any homework over the summer?"

"Nope," I said. "None."

"That's good," Jeffery said.

It was kind of awkward without Aunt Patty. "Where's Aunt Patty?"

"She's going to be at work for another two hours," Jeffery told me. "One of her employees just had her baby."

"Oh," I said, surprised. "Okay."

Then I had an idea.

"I'm going to the library in Aunt Patty's Sentra," I said without thinking.

"Library? But school's over," Jeffery said, chuckling.

Oops.

"Well, um . . ." I bit my bottom lip. "Um, I wanted to get the first book on my summer reading list."

There it is! I thought, nodding.

"Why are you nodding?" Jeffery asked, raising his eyebrows.

"I am? Whoops. Well, see you later," I spit out.

"Bye," Jeffery called as I shut the door.

In the tool shed I found the Sentra's keys and went to the car. I got in and started it up, getting excited.

I drove to the beach while listening to pop music. Without knowing it, I was dancing in time with the beats and it turned out that I was really happy to be going to visit Earth and the others.

I parked the car and walked across the beach, then the rocks. In the woods I pushed past some tree branches and bushes. Then I found the meadow.

In the middle was Storm and Water. The others were nowhere to be seen.

"April! You scared me to death! I thought you were somebody else," Water said. She trotted up to me.

"What are you doing here?" Storm asked, walking up behind Water.

"I came to visit," I said. "Where are the others?"

"Oh, Snow is trying to stop an avalanche in the Himalayas, Fire is cooling down a huge forest fire in the Smokey Mountains, and Earth is stopping an Earthquake in Asia somewhere," Water said.

"Oh," I said, nodding. "How long have they been gone?"

"About an hour," Storm said.

We talked for a few minutes but suddenly Water's mane and tail whipped up, splashing Storm and I.

"What's wrong?" Storm asked.

"I feel something," Water said. "But its not because of a disaster. It's . . . something else. But I don't know what."

"Do you feel vibrations?" Storm asked.

I looked at both of them, wondering what was going on.

"No. It's just . . ." Water trailed off, then completely froze. "Uh oh. Earth is in trouble."

"What?" I said.

"Earth's in trouble. I feel it," Water said, suddenly alarmed.

"Where is she?" Storm asked.

"Somewhere in Brazil," Water said. "She was trying to stop an earthquake but . . . something went wrong. She needs help!"

"I'm coming, too," I said. "That's my mother."

Water didn't bother to tell me that I wasn't supposed to call her that. She just knelt down and I got on.

"You're going to get wet, but it's better then getting electrocuted," Water said.

Sure enough, my shorts were soaked right away.

Water was fast. Storm was fast too. And I just clung on for dear life as Water whipped through the forest.

I wondered what happened to Earth. What *would* happen to her? She was a Spirit Horse, after all. What could nature do to her? She was trying to help people, and now she's hurt. That didn't make any sense to me.

If Earth got killed . . . well, then what? She was already a spirit. Would she stay in the horse body or go somewhere else? I leaned down to Water's ear.

"Is it possible for a Spirit Horse to get killed?" I whispered in her gray ear.

"Sometimes," Water answered. "It depends on how bad it is."

"How bad what is?" I asked. But Water slowed and we entered a tiny village. Dark skinned children ran around in dirty cloth. Women with the same darker skin had gorgeous headdresses and long, beaded necklaces. Their chocolate skin was spotless and their eyes were big and bright.

"Where are we?" I asked.

"Brazil," Water said. Storm came up behind Water and snorted.

"Can they see us?" I asked.

"No," Storm replied. "They can't."

"Okay," I said, sliding off Water's back. "Good."

"Well they can see you," Water said.

"Really?" I asked.

"You're not a Spirit Horse are you?" Storm asked, sarcasm in his voice. Grandpa's voice.

"Will it bother them?" I asked.

"No," Water said, shaking her head. Water flew everywhere.

"Okay," I said, nodding. "Good."

"Alright," Storm said. "I sense that she went this way." He started over to the left.

Water and I followed him. I walked awkwardly, my wet pants feeling like they were shrinking.

"Can I change into something else?" I asked, not being able to stand it anymore.

"Like what?" Water said.

"I don't know," I said. "But I don't think I can go on."

"Fine, here," Storm said, ripping a table cloth that was drying on a clothes line off the string.

I took the cloth and quickly changed, tying the fabric around my waist. It flowed all the way down to my ankles and was a dark red with gold stitching—no white, no see through. Good.

"Alright, I'm ready," I said.

We walked through the tiny village, many people pointed to me with awe. They all screeched and clapped their hands or just stared. I tried not to make too much eye contact in case I was going to get in trouble.

The wind picked up as we entered a small, dark alley in between two tan buildings. When the air whipped back my hair, I could hear a small, quiet whisper. At first I couldn't understand it, but after the second time, I got the message.

Follow the stars.

What? Follow stars? It was day time, no stars were out as far as I could see. I looked up. The sky was bright blue with little clouds swirled around. Birds flapped across the sun, casting large shadows on the pavement.

I looked in front of me, at Storm and Water. They walked silently. Did they hear the whisper too? I didn't think so, since they didn't bother to tell me in case I didn't hear it.

I didn't know if I should tell them. Did that whispering want me to? I had no clue. I decided to just keep my mouth shut for now and see what happens.

We came out of the alley. Something big was waiting for us.

Balloons filled the air, shouting and laughing was all I could hear.

They were having a festival.

"What's going on?" I asked, even though I already half-knew.

"I think they're celebrating something," Water said.

We passed men selling weird-looking foods like pig feet, goat heart, and lamb brain.

"Gross," I said, under my breath. I knew from history class that people from different countries didn't like when other people disrespected their food. But I couldn't help it. The sight of animals' intestines and the *smell* of it, oh gosh.

"Keep quiet, little one," Storm said. He chuckled.

"Sorry," I said.

We—well me, mostly—pushed past some people gathered around in a circle. From the distance I could make out a round, brown wheel. But I had no clue what it was.

A figure was attached to the wheel by its legs, and was dangling from thick rope above a blazing fire. We came closer.

And closer.

All three of us gasped when we saw what the figure was.

Earth.

VI

Save a Life

MY BREATHING STOPPED. People could see Earth? But how? She was a Spirit Horse, one that was invisible. Nobody saw Water and Storm this whole time. So what's wrong with Earth?

I screamed when I finally caught my breath and ran to the huge horse.

"Earth! Earth! Are you okay? Did they hurt you?" I rambled on.

Earth didn't answer. Her eyes were closed, and I thought she was already gone. But her large chest rose and fell slightly.

"Oh, thank goodness," I said, hugging her. The fire's flames grew huge, then died down. Then huge. Then small.

"We have to get her out," I told Water and Storm. "But how?"

Suddenly, two huge men wearing white cloth around their shaved heads grabbed my arms. They towed me away from Earth, blocking out the kicking and screaming.

"Let me go!" I yelled at them.

But they ignored me. Some more kicking and elbowing while being dragged away. Storm and Water tried to follow, the crowds of people were too much, and Earth needed them.

The muscular men dragged me a mile away from the crowds and into a tiny, tan building. It was dark and smelly.

"Where am I?" I asked.

One man said something, but I couldn't understand him.

The other guy said one word then helped the first man throw me into a dark cell. They locked me behind the iron bars and left without saying another word that I couldn't understand.

I sighed and looked around. In the cell was an old stool, a lantern, a very unpleasant hole that I thought might be the toilet, and a steel table with a matching cot.

I walked around in circles for a few minutes, thinking. What did I do? Disturb them? Wreck their celebration?

I didn't get it. Plus, I didn't get how they could see Earth if they couldn't see Water and Storm.

I decided that I needed to get out of here. For Earth. For mom. I walked around some more, thinking again. All I did was think. That was all I could do, really. I looked up at one of the walls. A big, blue star was painted on it. That gave me hope.

"Hmm," I said to myself, looking up more. There was a very high ceiling and no bars crossed over the top of the cell. The bars also didn't go up to the ceiling.

I pushed the heavy table to the bars and then lifted the stool on top. I stood on the stool carefully and kept my balance easily. Who knew getting out of jail was this easy? But actually, it wasn't.

Just as I was about to grip onto the top bar, a tiny buzz went to my ears. And more. I looked closely at the top bar. Small things, that looked like tiny spider legs, poked around the top of the bar. It was a electrified. I slowly backed down and took the stool off of the table. Then I just sat down and thought again.

So getting out of jail wasn't really that easy, I guess. But I had to help the Spirit Horses. Plus I had to get home to Aunt Patty! She was going to freak out and probably blame this all on poor Jeffery. I couldn't do that to him. But what about Earth? She's slowly frying in front of a huge crowd out there somewhere. She was the most important right now.

Gathering all my courage, I put the stool back on the table and stood on top of it. Then I grabbed the top bar and swung my legs over. I gave a blood curdling scream and dropped down.

I didn't know how long I was out for, but when I woke up, I was still in that tiny building. No one had heard me scream because I was so far away from town. What had I just done?

I looked at my hands. They were burned very badly and bleeding a lot.

I forced myself not to cry, even though tears were already running down my cheeks, and stood.

I found cloth in the old desk in the corner of the room and wrapped it around my burning, red flesh. I gritted my teeth, the pain on my hands almost too overwhelming. I felt like passing out again.

The white bandages quickly turned the color of my hands—red.

I found more and stuffed them down my shirt, the only place I could put them for now. I still had on the tablecloth from before. Since there was no clock or anything, I didn't know how long I had been out or how long it had been since I had seen Earth. But I knew I needed to hurry.

I stumbled out of the building and held my breath, praying for people to be around instead of a deserted area.

When I opened my eyes, all I could see was a shining, bright light and started sweating right away. The sun.

I put one of my injured hands above my eyes to shield away the white light and looked around. Very few people were wandering around. Some cleaned their faces and hands in a small stream. There were three small buildings, all tan like the other ones.

I opened and closed my mouth, just realizing that my tongue was very dry and that I was very thirsty. The sight of the stream water made my go crazy.

I ran over and was just about to dip my head in when a thought occurred to me.

"Is it safe to drink?" I asked an old woman with long, gray hair. She was scrubbing a young girl with the water.

She stared at me for a second, squinted, then glanced down at my hands. She gasped and then looked at me again. She nodded.

I gave her a small nod of thanks before drowning myself in the water. Yum.

The clear water was cold and refreshing. I gulped down as much as I could before I felt like it was going to come back up.

A small sound came from the woman. She was sitting in front of me now, on the other side of the stream.

She grunted again, pointed to me, then pointed to one of the small buildings.

"I can't," I said. "I have to go help someone."

The old woman frowned and shook her head. "Come," she barely got out the word.

I decided to follow her in to the building. Something about this women made me want to get to know her more.

Inside the building, three little kids—including the little girl the women was cleaning—ran around, screeching at each other.

"Hush!" The woman whispered.

The kids stopped and looked at her, but giggled and poked at each other some more.

The woman shook her head and smiled. Then she pointed to a chair. I sat down.

"Let," she said, reaching for my hands.

I hesitated, but gave them to her.

She carefully unwrapped the bandages and threw them away. Then she looked the bad burns over and nodded to herself. She got busy. After getting a small wooden bowl the lady put green paste in it along with white stuff, yellow stuff, and more green things. She stirred it with a wooden spoon and hummed softly as she did so. Then she added juice from a lemon and stirred some more. Finally, she came over and sat next to me with the bowl.

I flinched as she began rubbing the light green paste onto my burning hands, but then sighed happily. The paste cooled them down and I could see the flesh started to heal already.

"Thank you," I said to the lady. "That feels amazing." I didn't know if she spoke English, but I didn't care. As long as I said the words, I felt good about it.

But the lady nodded. "Heal."

"How long will it take?" I asked.

"Two," the woman said.

"Two days?" I said.

She shook her head, putting paste on my other hand. "Hour."

"Two hours? That's fantastic!" I said happily. "Thank you so much!"

"You're welcome," the lady said, smiling at me. She only had four teeth, but her smile was charming.

I gave her a small hug after she wrapped my hands with thin, cleaner bandages and thanked her again.

She gave me a nod and I walked out of her house and into the sun, already feeling a lot better. The burns were healing quickly and I started on my way. I was guessing the festival was toward the way the other houses were going, so I followed the path along the few houses. One house had a wind chime—the metal pieces were shaped like little gold stars. I smiled and kept on walking. The houses led me to a dark alley, and I ran through, not wanting to get caught by creeps.

I had to go through two other small villages before I heard the familiar shouts and grunts of the festival. I began to run, then stopped short.

What if they caught me again? I couldn't afford to get more burns.

I shook the bad thought away and continued toward the crowd. They barely noticed me as I pushed past them and stood in the front to see what was happening. Earth was still hanging by the ropes, her chest still rising and falling gently. But what I had just noticed was another Spirit Horse was there.

Fire.

He was standing silently next to Earth. His head was held high, his muzzle toward the air.

Why aren't they trying to capture him? I thought. Then I looked over to my right and saw Water and Storm. Right. The people could only see Earth for some reason.

I finally realized what Fire was doing. He was killing out the flames that were roasting Earth!

I wanted to cheer and clap for him, but then people would think I was doing that for Earth's dying. And I did not want that.

I went over to stand with Water and Storm. They watched Fire carefully. I mimicked them, not wanting to make them lose their concentration.

The flames were slowly dying away, and Fire was like a statue. A gorgeous statue. His chestnut body just *looked* hot and the flames coming from his neck and rump were blazing orange.

I held my breath as the fire finally died, thinking that someone would just make another. But then another sound came. But only me, Earth, Fire, Storm, and Water could hear it.

Snow bounded out of the bushes and stood on the other side of Earth. Then she posed just like Fire had, and I saw the ropes slowly freeze.

After a couple seconds the ropes were icicles. And then they broke from Earth's weight. Earth's fall sent screams through the crowd and they all ran like wild animals, in fear of Earth hurting them.

Snow and Fire had saved Earth and I didn't have to. Water and Storm couldn't of, even if they wanted to because they didn't have the right powers like Snow and Fire. But that was okay. As long as Earth was alright, nothing seemed to matter.

Earth stood up and shook her mane and tail. Dirt and ashes flew everywhere, showering the people who attempted to throw lassos around her neck again. Then she snorted, reared up on her hind legs, and galloped off. Water, Fire, Snow, Storm followed her.

"Wait!" I called. "What about me?"

Earth turned around and knelt down for me. "Hurry, little one."

"Okay, I'm good," I said, once I was on Earth's strong back.

"Ready?" Earth said.

"Yep," I replied, clinging on to Earth's brown and white mane.

And we were off.

VII

Target

WHEN WE GOT BACK TO THE Spirit Horses'
home, Chayania, aka the meadow, I slid off Earth's
back and gave her a huge hug.

"I'm so happy you're okay," I said. "I love you so
much."

"Me, too," Earth said, curling her neck around me.

"I have to go," I said. "Aunt Patty will be freaking
out."

"Oh, no she won't," Storm said. "When you're with us,
time slows down. Right now you've only been gone for an
hour and a half."

"Really? Wow," I said. "I guess that changes things. I
think I can be at the library for another half hour."

"What happened back there, Earth?" Water asked.

"I was trying to stop an earthquake, but something caught me," Earth said. "I don't know what it was but I couldn't stop it."

"It stopped your powers?" Snow asked. It surprised me that she was interested when she was usually snobby. Or maybe that was only with me.

"I think so," Earth said. "But it wasn't like I could use my powers to get me out of those ropes. The men who caught me stuck me with something and I fell asleep for a while.

"When I woke, I was dangling above a fire. I was there for about ten minutes before you guys showed up." Earth nodded toward Strom, Water, and me.

"How could they see you, though?" Fire said.

"I don't know," Earth replied. "It all happened so fast."

"That's very unusual," Storm said. "Spirit Horses are supposed to be invisible to all humans but the Cincinnati family."

"I know," Earth said. "I really don't know what happened back there."

"Well, it's done now," Water said. "Let's rest for a while."

They all knelt down, then plopped onto there bellies, their legs folded under their bodies.

"I guess I'll go" I said. "I'm not a huge fan of the library and Jeffery's probably getting suspicious."

"Alright, April," Earth said. "Have a good day."

"Bye, guys," I said. "Can I visit tomorrow?"

"Sure," Water said. "We love your company."

I just barely got out of Chayania when I heard Snow sigh and I knew she was rolling her eyes at Water's comment.

At home, Jeffery was making lunch. I sat down and sighed heavily.

"Wow, what a day at the library!" I said, glancing at Jeffery.

Jeffery turned to me. "How'd it go?"

"Wonderful," I replied. "I got my first book, and got in four chapters."

"That's great," Jeffery said. "Hungry?"

"Starving," I said, patting my stomach.

"Here you are," Jeffery said. He put a huge burger on a paper plate with bacon, cheese, lettuce, and tomato. Then he dumped a pile of potato chips onto the other side of the plate and put it in front of me. "Drink?"

"Cranberry juice, please," I said, chomping on a chip.

Jeffery filled a plastic cup and slid it over to me. "Enjoy. I have to go organize Miss Patty's bills."

"Thanks," I said, taking a huge bite of the burger.

Yum.

Aunt Patty came home a few hours later and we ate dinner. Jeffery out did himself tonight—prime rib, a tossed salad, and his creamy mashed potatoes with sour cream and bacon bits.

After dinner, I went right to bed. I wanted to get lots of sleep for tomorrow when I met up with the Spirit Horses.

The next morning I woke up and got dressed quickly.

After breakfast I told Aunt Patty I was going to Sasha's to give her the summer reading list.

"Can't you just text it to her?" Aunt Patty had asked.

"No," I said. "We're best friends, Aunt Patty. We have to see each other and just hang out for a while."

Aunt Patty had raised her eyebrows, but nodded. "Just be home by one."

I walked out of the huge mansion and walked to the Sentra. Then I drove to the boardwalk, crossed the beach, and entered the woods when no one was looking.

I staggered over some rocks and tripped over some over-grown roots a couple of times, but finally entered Chayania.

I stopped where I stopped before.

Only one was there—Earth.

"Where is everybody?" I screeched, running over.

Earth didn't look the same. The brightness to her liquid brown eyes were gone, the happy flick of her tail wasn't there—her tail laid limp and lifeless.

"April, get on," Earth said, kneeling.

I got on and decided to wait to ask questions when we were moving.

When Earth stood up and began cantering toward the woods, all the words poured out.

"Where is everybody? What happened? Are you okay? What happened to everyone else?" I asked.

"April," Earth said. Her voice was quiet and the cheerfulness was gone like her bright eyes. "I don't know what happened. But I do know it's something with Water. The others are already trying to help her—I agreed to stay here and wait for you."

"Where is Water?" I asked.

"Australia," Earth replied. "She was stopping a tsunami when she was caught by humans."

"Humans? Again?"

"Yes, I'm afraid so," Earth said. "We don't know what's happening."

"How can they see you guys?" I asked.

"I don't know," Earth said.

"I thought you were supposed to be invisible," I mumbled.

"We are," Earth said. "But the humans are making something that makes them able to see us."

"Like what? And how do they know you're here?"

"Well, I think it's because some of the other Spirit Horses are making it noticeable that there are no more natural disasters and now the humans are suspicious," Earth said.

"How is that a bad thing? I mean, having no more natural disasters," I said.

"Scientists," Earth said. "They think something's wrong with the planet."

"Oh," I said.

Earth slowed and knelt down so I could get off. We were in a dry place. Desert.

"Where are we?" I asked.

"The Victorian Desert," Earth told me. "We must travel quickly to save Water."

"Do you need to rest?" I asked, wiping my thighs. My shorts are caked with dirt.

"A little," Earth said. "Just so I have enough energy to help the others."

I nodded. "Okay."

We sat for a little while, talking. It felt like old times. Before mom and dad died. Before my life had changed forever.

Earth told me about the other Spirit Horses.

There is another group of Spirit Horses—the O' Donnell family. There is Flower, Camouflage, Cloud, and Dusty. They are the second Spirit Horse group, after the Cincinnati's, of course. They helped people around the world, too, but for different reasons. Plus, they covered around the tropical islands like Hawaii, Fiji, and Guam.

The other group is the Marshall family. Their names are Roots and Vines. They didn't have many dead family members yet. They covered the densely populated areas.

Finally, I got back on Earth and we headed to Water and the others.

We ended up in a small city, nothing compared to Brazil.

People were everywhere, though. Huge crowds of people huddled in front of different carts that had coffee, clothes, jewelry, and different foods.

"I've always wanted to come to Australia," I said. "But right now it's for the wrong reason."

"I agree," Earth said, nodding.

"Where do you think they are?" I asked.

"Somewhere," Earth said.

I didn't hear any sarcasm in her tone and knew she was truly worried about her best friend Water. What could have happened to her?

"Follow the stars," I whispered.

"What's that?" Earth asked.

"Nothing," I said quietly.

We walked through the city, looking everywhere for Water and the others. But all we saw was more people, stands, and animals like goats and pigs. "Can't you like send a message to them?" I asked.

Earth laughed. "No. It's not that simple."

We walked across a small bridge that was crossed over a small brook. I thought about the stars. I looked for stars everywhere, but couldn't find any. Was the star the same sign for Water as it was for Earth? I didn't know. But if I found out, I could be looking for something other then stars.

"Help," I whispered.

The wind responded by blowing past us, then whispering, *Take a walk on the wild side.*

Take a walk on the wild side?

What was that supposed to mean? I had no clue. I didn't want to ask Earth in case I wasn't supposed to. I wasn't much of a risk-taker. Well, except for burning my hands off to get out of the Brazilian jail.

I thought about the clue from the wind. What did that mean? I thought about it for awhile as we walked. Wild side could mean anything—animals, dares, dangerous things. Take a walk didn't really mean much to me except for what it sounded like—taking a walk.

We walked past a small crowd of people waiting in front of a gate. A guy with bushy blond hair and an Australian accent was on a stand, hollering into a megaphone.

"Ladies and gentleman!" the guy shouted. "Today is the grand opening of the Greenway Zoo! We have your lions, your tigers, your zebras. All the regulars. But now we have a special animal—a giant horse! Make sure to check out the giant horse in the center. Have a nice day and enjoy the zoo."

Then it hit me. *Wild animals.*

Giant horse.

Water was put in the zoo!

"Earth! Earth," I said. "Water is the giant horse! We have to go get her."

"Yes, lets go," Earth said.

"Wait, I'll have to pay," I said, disappointed. What if Earth wanted to go alone and leave me here? I didn't want that!

"Who pays these days?" Earth said.

I paused. "Well, everyone."

Earth chuckled. "Get on." She knelt down and I climbed onto her back.

Then she backed up, leaned back, and exploded. We were going so fast I couldn't even catch my breath. I finally saw what we were heading for—the twelve foot high metal gate and the crowd of people.

"Earth, wait! No!" I cried, but it was too late. Earth sprung up on her hind legs and leaped into the air. It seemed like we were in slow motion as I wrapped my arms around her thick neck and clamped my legs down, determined not to fall. She cleared the crowd and it looked like she was about to fall straight down, but she kept on going. Then she cleared the gate. And landed cleanly on the other side, just after a couple of girls who screeched and ran.

But why? I thought they couldn't see Earth anymore.

"Why are they running?" I asked. "I thought you were invisible."

"I am," Earth said. "But *you* aren't."

"Oh, yeah," I said.

I turned. People were everywhere, crowding around us. But all they saw was a girl floating in the air.

"Um, Earth?" I said. "Can we go now?"

"Yes," Earth said. She turned and began to gallop away from the crowd. You could hear the "wows" and the gasping as the people watched me float away.

"That's funny," I said to myself, looking at the crowd. I couldn't help but wave and give them a bright smile as Earth carried me away.

They all gasped again.

I laughed and shook my head. "Birdbrains."

We passed lots of animals—lions, bears, birds, rodents, and camels. But the most I could see were monkeys. They were *everywhere!* There was probably fifteen different kinds of monkeys in the zoo. But we finally stopped in the center of the zoo and started searching.

"Water!" I called. People turned to stare at me but I didn't care. "Water, where are you?"

The bushes behind us rustled and Fire, Snow, and Storm came out. "We know where she is," Fire said.

"Really? Where?" I asked eagerly.

"Follow us," Snow said.

They turned and trotted through some bushes and Earth followed.

We came out in front of a hexagon-shaped cage filled with trees and leaves. All I could see was green. Green, green, green!

But I still searched for a spot of gray to indicate that Water really was in there.

Crowds of people gathered around, searching for the hidden "giant horse". They were so into looking for the animal, they didn't notice me.

"I think I can fit through the bars," I told Earth.

"Try," she said.

I slid down and sneaked around the cage where no one was. Then I tested out the space between the iron bars. I could probably make it if I sucked in.

I slid through, holding my breath. Then I made myself disappear into the trees so no one would catch me. There were so many bushes and leaves I could barely see where I was going. But I pushed them out of the way and finally stumbled into the middle of the cage where there was a circle of dirt and a small pool of water. And in the middle of the dirt was Water.

"Hey! You're here! Are you alright?" I asked, kneeling down beside her.

She coughed. "Not really, April," she said.

"What's wrong?" I asked.

"They drained my powers," Water coughed.

"How though? They can do that?"

"Apparently," Water said.

"So how are you going to get out of here?" I asked. "You need to get out—you're not just a zoo animal like all the others."

"No, I'm not," Water said. "But I don't see how I can get out. I can barely stand."

"I'll be right back," I said. I left the cage and snuck over to the other Spirit Horses.

"How is she?" Storm asked, obviously the most concerned one.

"She said the humans drained her powers," I told them.

"What?" Fire asked.

"That's what she said," I repeated.

"So she can't get out?" Earth asked.

"No," I said sadly. "She told me she could barely stand."

"That's not good," Storm said, beginning to pace.

"Don't worry," I said. "We'll get her out."

"Yes, we will," Earth said. "We're not leaving her."

"Of course not," Fire said.

Everything was silent for a moment. That's when I realized Snow wasn't with us anymore.

"Where's Snow?" I asked.

"Umm . . . . she's right there," Storm said, pointing his nose behind him. "Isn't she?"

"No," I said. "She's not there. I don't see her."

"Me either," Fire said. "Where would she go?"

I thought for a moment. "Wait. I think I know." I left them and went back to the cage. I slipped through and found the center again. Water was in the same spot, but Snow stood in front of her, her head raised high, her tail spread out, a slight glow going over her body.

"What are you doing?" I hissed.

Nobody answered. Snow stayed in the same position.

"What's she doing?" I asked Water. But Water's eyes were closed and for a second I thought she was dead.

"Water!" I screeched and ran to the giant horse, clutching her neck. "Water, wake up! Don't die . . . . again!"

Water's body rose up and I was forced to let go of her neck.

She spread out her legs and went back down, landing on her hooves. Her bright eyes opened and her mane began to flow with water as did her tail.

Snow came out of her position. But she looked weaker. Her coat was no longer a blinding white, but more of a really light gray. Her mane and tail weren't as free anymore and her blue eyes sagged a little.

"What happened?" I asked.

Water answered. "She gave me half her power so I could live."

I couldn't believe it. Snow, cousin Jillian, being nice? Well, I guess being nice was easy for her if I wasn't the one she was talking to.

"So are you alright now?" I asked.

"Yes, I'm well enough," Water replied. She turned to Snow. "Thank you very much Snow."

Snow dipped her head down to Water, but didn't look too good.

"Are you okay, Snow?" I asked quietly. I expected a mean response, but Snow just nodded.

"Yeah," she barely got out. "I'm fine." She hobbled around me and used her freezing power to freeze the bars, then shatter them. She easily stepped through them and walked away. I stared after her.

"Come on, little one," Water said.

I followed her out.

We went back to Chayania slowly. Snow couldn't do more then a slow canter and everyone wanted to wait for her, including me. Back in the meadow Snow fell in a heap of light gray. The others gathered around her, but Earth stayed with me.

"Is she alright?" I asked the brown and white horse.

"I think she'll be okay," Earth said. "But we'll keep a close eye on her, alright?"

I nodded. "Okay."

"Why don't you head home? You look tired," Earth said.

"Yeah," I said, nodding. "I better go. Good luck."

"Come back anytime," Earth called.

"I will," I said. And I walked through the meadow and out of the gorgeous Chayania, leaving a weak Snow behind.

VIII

Get it Out

FOR THE NEXT THREE DAYS I couldn't visit Chayania and the Spirit Horses because I had been too busy. Now I was getting ready to go over Alicia's house. I packed a sleepover bag and went to the bathroom to get my toothbrush and hairbrush.

"Alicia's here," I called to Aunt Patty after I heard the car honking.

"Bye, sweetie!" Aunt Patty replied. "Have fun."

"Bye," I said before shutting the door behind me.

I ran to Alicia's car and opened the door.

"Hey," Alicia said as I slid into the car seat. "How's it going?"

"Good," I said. "You?"

"Fine," Alicia said. "I haven't seen you in forever!"

"I know," I said. "So, are we going to get Sasha?"

"Yup," Alicia said, nodding. "She said she'll be ready in ten minutes. So we're going to Kate's to get a burger, okay?"

"Good, I'm starving," I said. "I didn't have time to eat lunch."

"Remember this: Sasha wants a double cheeseburger with tomato, small fry, and a large Sprite," Alicia said. "I forget easily. Actually, I'm surprised I remembered to tell you!"

I laughed. "I'll remember it."

Alicia drove out of the driveway and headed toward the drive-through restaurant. "So, what's up with you?"

I sat up. "What do you mean?"

"You haven't answered my texts in the past week until yesterday."

"Oh," I said flatly. What did I tell her? If I said I was too busy to look at my phone, she would ask what I was doing. And I couldn't tell her that. I promised Earth I wouldn't give away their secret. But I started sweating so I blurted out, "I haven't been feeling well."

"Really? What's wrong?" Alicia asked.

I gulped. "Um, I had a stomach ache. I could barely get out of bed. Jeffery had to serve me my food in my bed."

"Oh," Alicia said, frowning. "But you feel better now, right?"

"Of course," I said.

She smiled. "Good! Tonight is going to be awesome."

She pulled up to the drive-through and placed our orders. Then we paid and got our food.

I called Sasha.

"Hello?"

"Sash, you ready?" I asked.

"Yup! I'm waiting outside," Sasha said.

"Okay, we'll be there in five minutes," I said.

"Okay, bye," Sasha said.

We hung up.

At Alicia's house we sat down at the kitchen table and ate our food. I felt so guilty about lying to one of my best friends. We told each other everything—and I mean *everything*. Even when Sasha accidentally stole a pair of sunglasses she didn't hide it from us.

"Guys," I said. "I need to tell you something."

My friends looked at me expectantly. I gulped.

IX

The Truth

I COULDN'T BELIEVE I HAD DONE this. I had betrayed The Spirit Horses. Would they ever forgive me? I didn't know. But I hoped they would. I needed to hear mom's voice—I couldn't lose that a second time. I needed to hear dad's horrible jokes. I already lost those things once, and now I was afraid of losing them again. But I couldn't keep lying to my closest friends—it wasn't fair to them.

Now Alicia's shaky hands gripped the steering wheel as she drove the car into the boardwalk's parking lot. She parked, shut the car off, and unbuckled her seat belt.

"I can't believe this," Alicia said, leaning her head back. "Why would you say that stuff?"

I suddenly went on defensive. "Because it's true!" I shouted.

"No it's not, April," Sasha said calmly from the back seat. "Listen, I—"

"No, *you* listen!" I growled.

Sasha jerked her head back.

"You want to see I'm not lying? Follow me," I said, slamming the car door after sliding out.

The girls followed me out. I sped-walked through the boardwalk, onto the beach, over the sharp rocks, and finally, into the woods.

"Where are we?" Alicia asked.

I didn't answer.

Instead, I led them through the bushes. I stopped, Alicia and Sasha stopped behind me, and I swallowed hard.

Then I pushed the greens out of the way and stepped into Chayania.

All of the horses were there. Snow was still lying down, her coat slowly turning a darker gray. Fire stood beside her and Water laid down next to her. Storm stood with Fire and Earth . . . . was walking right over to me.

She looked at me straight in the eyes, her liquid brown eyes seemed to tell a story. Tears filled my eyes as I nodded once.

Then she turned her back on me, swished her tail slightly, and walked to the others.

I waved my friends to come out from the bushes.

Their reactions were what I expected—mouths open, eyes wide, gasps coming from their mouths.

"Told you," I whispered to them.

And I walked away from them, not caring where they went next or if they left me without a ride home. But they just stood still as I walked slowly to the giant horses.

Summer Solstice~Spirit Horses

I had seen the disappointment in Earth's eyes. I felt the disappointment in mine. But I couldn't keep lying to Alicia and Sasha.

I stopped in front of the horses and sighed quietly. They all looked at me, as if they were expecting me to say something. And I did.

"Guys, I'm really sorry," I said. "But I couldn't keep this huge secret from my closet friends. Can you forgive me? Please?"

Fire studied my face, then gave one small nod. "I do."

Everyone followed him, even Snow. They all said two simple words: I do.

"Thank you! Thank you," I said. I ran to hug them, but stopped. I didn't want more burns from Fire or shocks from Storm. So I settled on a bright smile.

"Why don't you bring your friends over here?" Earth said.

"Guys!" I called. "Alicia, Sasha."

They both slowly walked over and gave tense smiles to the Spirit Horses.

"Hi," Alicia said shyly.

"Hello," Sasha said.

"Hello, girls," Earth said, stepping forward. "April has informed us that she has let out the secret of us to you girls. We hope you can keep this secret safe inside you."

"We will," Sasha said, speaking for Alicia as well.

"Good. And thank you," Earth said. "Why don't you step forward, and I'll introduce you to the family."

Sasha and Alicia stepped forward and smiled.

"This is Fire," Earth said. Fire stepped up. "His ability is to stop wild fires, but don't touch him because he can give you serious burns. Next, Water." Water stepped forward. "Her ability is to stop hurricanes and floods. If you touch her, you can count on getting soaked." Storm came out from behind Snow. "This is Storm. He stops tornados and can control lightening. And that is Snow on the grass. She can stop avalanches and can freeze and thaw out many things. Right now, she is weak because she helped Water escape a problem by giving her half her power." Earth took a giant step forward. "And I am Earth. I stop earthquakes."

"Nice to meet you all," Alicia said.

"Yes, nice to meet you," Sasha added.

"The same," Storm said, giving them both a slight nod.

"How's Snow?" I asked.

"She's not looking too good, I'm afraid," Earth said.

"Why? What's wrong?" I asked, even though I already had a sense of the answer.

"Since she gave away some of her power to Water," Earth explained, "she has been weak. Now her power has been drained from her, and she can't move much."

"Why has it been drained?" I demanded.

"We don't know," Fire said.

"How come?" I asked.

"April," Water said, "you need to understand that we don't know what's happening. We really don't. If we did, we would be helping her out."

I finally calmed down. "Okay, okay. I'm sorry."

"It's fine, April," Fire said.

"So, are you going to try to figure out how to help her?" I asked.

"Of course," Storm said. "We're trying our hardest."

"Good," I said. "Now we better get home." I waved toward Alicia and Sasha.

"Goodbye," Earth said. "We'll see you soon."

"Right," I said, nodding.

Alicia, Sasha, and I walked out of Chayania and went back to Alicia's house with little words.

X

A Water Day

ALICIA, SASHA, AND I CHECKED on Snow almost everyday. Aunt Patty, Alicia's mom, and Sasha's mom were all suspicious about why we wanted to hang out with each other so much. We used every excuse in the book—we need to help each other with book reports, we were bored, we wanted to share ideas about Sasha's birthday party. All of them always asked, why can't you just text them?

One day at Chayania, the three girls stood beside a laying-down Snow. Earth was talking to them.

"Girls, Snow isn't looking much better," Earth said. "We need to find a good source of power for her."

"But where?" I asked.

Earth's nose wrinkled. "I'm not sure. But we need to start looking. So, Fire and Storm go south. Water and I will take the girls north and we'll look there. Snow, I'll have Rags look after you."

"Who's Rags?" Sasha asked.

"Rags!" Earth called.

Out of the bushes a huge deer, three times the size of a normal one, like the horses, scampered out. He had large antlers on top of his head.

"Yes?" he said in a deep voice.

Earth looked at him. "Will you watch Snow for a while?"

Rags looked at Snow then back at Earth. "Sure. What's the problem?"

"Snow's losing her power," Water told him.

"That's horrible!" Rags cried. "Of course I'll stay with her."

"Thank you," Earth said, dipping her head. "We really appreciate it."

"Of course, of course," Rags replied, laying down next to Snow.

Snow's coat was now a dark gray, like Water's, but it wasn't dappled. Her mane was now getting darker. Her eyes drooped down, the skin around her bones seemed to shrink and cling to them more. Snow actually was getting smaller and smaller.

"Let's go," Fire said to Storm. When the boys had galloped off, Earth and Water knelt down.

"Alright, your either getting dirty or wet," Water said.

"I'll go on Earth," I said. "You two can go on Water."

Alicia and Sasha nodded.

It wasn't that I didn't want to get wet, but that I wanted to feel closer to my mother more. Earth and I had a special connection that nobody could understand. Even Alicia and Sasha.

"Alright, let's get moving," Water said, kneeling down.

Alicia and Sasha were silent as they stared at Water.

"Get on," I whispered to them.

"Oh!" Sasha said. She walked over to Water and climbed onto her back, followed by Alicia.

Earth knelt down and I quickly hopped on, then gathered her thick mane in my hands.

"Everybody ready?" Earth asked.

Alicia and Sasha nodded. I said, "Yup. Let's go get Snow power!"

Earth and Water went off, galloping into the forest. The trees were just blurs as the giant horses ran through. I looked over at Sasha and Alicia. Their mouths were open, eyes wide, Sasha's hand gripping Water's mane, Alicia's arms wrapped around Sasha, clinging on for dear life.

I stifled a laugh and focused between Earth's pointed ears. We were still in the forest.

"Where are we going?" I asked her.

"You'll see soon," she replied.

We went on for another five minutes before Earth and Water slowed. They stopped in front of a gorgeous waterfall.

I hopped down after Earth knelt down on her knees and walked around her, trying to get a good look at the beautiful waterfall.

"Where are we?" Sasha breathed as she slid down from Water's back.

"Prunea," Water answered. "This is our secret waterfall."

"Yes, and we think if we search hard enough we can find Snow's power," Earth said.

"Really? You think so?" I asked.

"I'm pretty sure," Earth said.

Alicia got off of Water, her pants soaked. "So, where should we start?"

"Um, you girls can start by the water, we'll take the forest," Water said.

"Okay," I replied, walking over to the waterfall.

Alicia and Sasha followed me, their walks funny because of their wet jeans. My jeans wear caked with dirt, but it didn't matter, anyway.

"Let's start over here," I said.

"Alright," Alicia agreed. She followed me over to a large rock next to the water.

"What are we supposed to be looking for?" Sasha asked. "I mean, what does "power" look like?"

I thought for a second. "Um, I don't really . . . know."

"Should we ask?" Alicia said, nodding toward the Spirit Horses.

"No," I said, shaking my head. "I don't want to bother them. Let's just look."

"Okay," Sasha said.

We looked behind rocks, in the water, inside of animals' burrows. But we didn't find anything interesting. It didn't help that we didn't know what to look for exactly.

I stopped looking behind a bush when the wind whipped through my hair.

Look within the deep waters.

"What?" I whispered to myself.

"What's wrong, April?" Alicia called over to me.

I stood up straight and fumbled over my words. "Um, nothing, I . . . I was just talking . . . to myself . . ."

Alicia looked at me with a weird look, but continued to look in the shallow waters of the waterfall.

I sat on a small rock and thought for a moment.

Look within the deep waters. So, obviously, it had something to do with the waterfall sense it said waters. But where in the water? Did the wind want me to swim deep down in the water? I didn't really want to, but if it meant finding Snow's power, I had to.

I took a deep breath and dove into the cool water from the rock I was sitting on.

The water hit me hard and I could barely open my eyes in the fresh water. But I forced them open so I could see where I was going since I didn't have goggles.

There were tiny silver fish that swam around the sharp rocks at the bottom. I guessed I was probably twelve feet down when I felt the hard bottom.

I held my breath, though, and swam around some rocks, scaring more silver fish out into the open. I pushed over some smaller rocks, searching for something interesting. But all I found was dirt, more fish, and underwater plants.

All the time I was looking, I forgot about my breathing. Suddenly, I saw black spots in my vision and franticly waved my arms and kicked my feet, trying to get to the surface. But on the way up I hit my head on something hard. A rock?

I didn't know because I was already gone.

My eyes opened and all I saw was white. Snow? Had she gotten her power back? I swung my arms around, trying to reach her, but they never got to her cold body.

Then I realized where I was. I was in my room at Aunt Patty's mansion, staring at the white ceiling. My head hurt so bad—whenever I tilted it to the side, I gave out a slight cry.

What happened? The last thing I remembered was being in the water. Trying to get to the surface, trying to live . . . .

Someone knocked on my door.

My voice was hoarse as I called, "Come in."

Aunt Patty opened the door, her face creased with worry lines. "How are you?" she whispered.

"Fine," I barely got out. I tried to sit up, but my back ached like my head. "What happened?"

Aunt Patty sat on the end of my bed. "Alicia and Sasha said you guys were walking down Main street to get supper and you tripped and hit your head on a fire hydrant. They had brought you to the hospital and called me."

"Oh," I croaked. Of course they had lied. They had to.

"So, how are you feeling?"

"My head hurts," I said. "And I can't sit up."

"The doctor said you had a spinal injury somehow," Aunt Patty told me. "And you had to get fifteen stitches on your forehead."

I felt my head and found there was a bandage wrapped around my forehead.

"So, tomorrow," Aunt Patty said, "you're going to get spinal surgery."

The word *surgery* made me freeze. "Surgery?"

Aunt Patty nodded.

"Why?" I demanded.

"Calm down, April," Aunt Patty said softly. "The doctor said your spine isn't aligned right. He needs to fix it."

I probably hit my back on a rock, too, I thought. I didn't just hit my head—I had disappeared into the deep and landed on dozens of sharp rocks.

"Aunt Patty . . ." I wanted to talk more, but my brain said something else.

And I slipped into a deep sleep.

XI

The Three "S's"

I STAYED IN BED ALL DAY, EVEN though I asked Aunt Patty if I could get up. She always said no. So Jeffery brought me lunch and dinner and anything else I wanted like magazines, books, or a notebook and pen.

The next day, the eighteenth, was probably the scariest day in my life.

Surgery day.

Nothing was more disturbing then people going into your body with tools and putting you to sleep. I had never had surgery before, and I never thought I would have to have it.

I never had any broken bones or any serious illnesses that made doctors concerned.

Aunt Patty helped me get dressed and helped me into the wheelchair Jeffery had got for me since I could barely walk. Then we borrowed a special van so I wouldn't have to get out of the wheel chair, and headed to the hospital.

QUINTON MEMORIAL HOSPITAL was printed on the huge brick building with dark, thick letters. I gulped as Aunt Patty pushed my wheelchair through the hospital automatic doors. Right away the hospital smell came to me—flowers for get better gifts, medicines, and . . . . death.

People say the safest place for sick people is the hospital but don't they know that a lot of people also *die* in hospitals? Because whatever the doctors do don't work, and they slip away in the "safest" place, thinking they were safe in the doctors' hands.

I hoped I was safe here.

A few hours later after surgery, I laid in the stiff hospital bed, still as I've ever been. I hated stitches—I always thought they would rip out if I moved an inch. So I stayed on that bed, even when the nurses asked me if I wanted to walk around for a couple minutes to get feeling in my legs.

When Aunt Patty came into the room, she smiled and gave me a gentle hug. "How you feeling?"

"Alright, I guess," I said.

"It wasn't that big of a deal, now was it?" Aunt Patty asked, chuckling.

"Well, I wasn't here for almost all of it," I said. "So I guess it was alright."

"Good," Aunt Patty said. "Jeffery told me to bring you this." She took a container out of her purse and gave it to me after taking of the lid.

I reached in without looking and found one of Jeffery's special peanut butter brownies on my palm. I took a bite.

"Yummy," I replied, eating the rest of it. "Tell Jeffery I said thank you."

"I think you can," Aunt Patty said. "The doctors said you're doing so well right now, you can come home in a few hours."

"Really?" I exclaimed. "I'm definitely ready to get out of here."

"I think so too," Aunt Patty replied. "I have to take a short trip to work, but I'll be back at five-thirty to pick you up."

"Okay," I said, looking at the giant wall clock in my boring-colored room. It was almost two-thirty.

"See you later," Aunt Patty said. She knelt down, kissed my forehead, and left.

I drifted off to sleep for about a half hour, then woke to the sound of girls' voices outside my room.

"Is she sleeping?" Someone said.

"I don't know," another girl said. "I don't want to wake her up."

"Should we check?"

I finally realized it was Alicia and Sasha out there. I tried my best to clear my throat.

"Come in!" I called.

They didn't hear me because they still argued if I was sleeping or not. So I tried again.

"Guys, come in!" I shouted.

Finally, the door opened slowly and Sasha popped her head in.

"Oh, she's awake!" she said. "Come on, Alicia."

"Are you sure?" Alicia asked.

"Yeah." Sasha opened the door more, then walked inside. "Her eyes are open, aren't they?" she added, rolling her eyes.

"Hey," Alicia said softly to me. "How you doing?"

"Fine," I said. I took a sip of water from the plastic cup on the metal tray next to my bed.

"That wasn't the best day, huh?" Sasha said, sitting on the end of the bed.

"Nope," I said, grinning and shaking my head. "I wasn't really looking forward to surgery."

"We know," Alicia said. "And we felt so bad. But why did you go under so far?" She whispered the last sentence.

"I don't know," I said. Did I tell them what I heard from the wind? I remembered I told them about Earth and the others because I didn't want to lie, so why was this such a big deal?

"Yes, you do," Sasha said. "Something happened."

"What was it?" Alicia pressed. "Tell us."

"I don't know if I can," I said.

"Why?" Sasha asked.

"I don't know," I replied quietly.

They sighed.

"I'm sorry," I mumbled. "Fine, I'll tell you."

They waited, staring at me. I swallowed hard, still unsure. But I went on.

"First, when Earth was captured the wind, or something in the wind, told me to follow the stars. Then, when Water was in trouble, it told me to walk on the wild side. And then we found the zoo. And two days ago, when we were looking for Snow's power, it told me to look in the deep waters."

Alicia slowly nodded. "So . . ."

"So I was listening to the wind the whole time," I said. "Because it worked the last two times."

Sasha began to nod. "I get it."

"You do?" I asked hopefully. "Really?"

"Yeah," Sasha said. "Plus, you were just trying to help Snow. You didn't know that you'd get hit with those rocks. It's not your fault at all."

I smiled. "Yeah. If I knew getting hit by those sharp rocks was a huge possibility, I probably wouldn't have done that."

"No, you probably still would," Alicia said, laughing. "Nothing stops you."

I joined her. "Yeah, that's true."

The door opened and Sue, one of the nurses, popped her head in. "Girls, you have five minutes until April needs to rest."

"Alright," Sasha said. "We'll be out."

"I don't want you guys to leave," I told them. "I'm not even tired."

"We don't want to leave either, but that nurse looks like she knows how to fight," Alicia said, teasing.

"Okay, okay," I said. "I'll see you guys in a few days?"

"Of course," Sasha said.

"And then we'll find Snow's power," I said firmly.

Alicia and Sasha looked at each other.

"What?" I asked. "Is something wrong with Snow?"

"Well, no," Alicia said. "But we don't think you should be looking for stuff like that when you just got stitches in two different places."

"I'm fine," I snapped. "And I'm going to help Snow."

"Okay," Sasha said, giving up. "We're leaving now."

"Bye," I said, turning my back on them.

They left and closed the door slowly. What did they mean, I couldn't help out? It was my family, after all. Not theirs. Plus, I was completely fine. If I was leaving today, how could I *not* be fine?

XII

Breaking Rules

O N THE TWENTIETH, ALSO KNOWN as the Summer Solstice, I laid in my bed at home, thinking. It was barely eight-thirty and the boardwalk didn't open until ten. But I had to get to Chayania and help out Snow. I had to get her power back for her.

Also, how was I going to get out of here? Aunt Patty was at work, sure, but Jeffery was here. He was watching me like a hawk to make sure I did no "funny-business" as he and Aunt Patty called it. I felt much better, not feeling the stitches in my back or head at all. The doctor said I had to come back soon so he could take them out, and I couldn't wait.

Around nine-thirty, I rolled over and got out of bed. Then I took probably twenty minutes trying to get on new clothes. Finally, I threw my hair up into a bun and opened my window. The air was hot but a cool breeze came through.

I looked down, seeing only dark green grass. The grass was cushy, but I didn't want to risk getting more surgery. I dropped five pillows down, off my bed and from the hall closet. Then I lowered myself out the window and onto the roof. My plan was to get as close to the ground as I could, then just drop onto the pillows.

The plan kind of went the right way. I mean, I did land on the pillows. But before that I lost my grip and rolled down the roof. But I still landed on the pillows, which was good. I only felt a little pain that shot up my spine, but fought through it and stood. I hid the pillows in the tool shed and got the keys to Aunt Patty's quietest car. Then I got in it, started it, and hoped Jeffery didn't hear it. He didn't.

I drove out of the driveway and started to the beach. As I drove, I felt my spine begin to ache. My head started to hurt to, and when I reached my hand up to feel the rough stitches, it came back down with blood.

"Ugh!" I mumbled, rummaging through the glove compartment for a napkin. I found one, kept it on my forehead, and ignored the weird looks people gave me when they drove by my car.

When I got to the beach, I parked and slowly slid out of the red car. Then I walked across the boardwalk and went straight to the forest.

I climbed over the rocks, thinking about Alicia and Sasha. I didn't mean to snap at them, but how could they say that to me?

And as I peeked around the bushes that opened up into Chayania, I saw them. Talking to the Spirit Horses.

Alicia sat cross-legged on the ground, next to Snow who was still getting darker. Sasha was walking next to Earth and Water, who looked as if they were showing Sasha different things in Chayania. Fire and Storm weren't there—they were probably still looking for Snow's power.

I decided not to say anything to Alicia and Sasha. If they saw me, they would probably send me straight home. So I snuck behind some trees and slowly walked to Chayania's waterfall.

Then a thought occurred to me—can't the Spirit Horses sense I'm here? Great. Just great. But I shook the thought out of my head and kept walking. If they did, I didn't care. I would just deal with it when it happened. Well, *if* it happened.

And it didn't. I kept hiding behind trees, bushes, and giant plants. Nobody ever noticed me and they never stopped what they were doing. I was surprised Alicia and Sasha were so comfortable with Earth, Water, and Snow without me. I wondered if they wanted me to know that they visited today.

Would they even tell me?

Finally, I got to the waterfall. The gorgeous clear water was not loud at all—it was almost silent. Flamingoes stood in the shallow end, some with one leg cocked up. I smiled at them because I never really saw a Flamingo this close before. Yeah, maybe at the zoo but they were always behind bars. Like jail.

I walked around some large rocks. I knew exactly what I had to do.

I dove into the cold water and swam to the end, where the water splashed into the pool. I quickly went through the wall of water, and was now inside the waterfall it seemed like.

Behind the water wall was not just more solid rock. It was actually a small cave-like thing. I swam over to a single rock and lifted myself onto it. Then I risked falling into the water and getting hit by rocks again by leaping off of the rock and grabbing for the cave's ledge.

I made it.

I clambered onto the brown rock, trying to get a good grip. I got the grip, lifted myself up, and rolled over onto the rock.

"Yes," I whispered to myself.

I crawled into the cave more, squinting for light. Now I wished I brought a flashlight. But I wouldn't be able to get out of the house with Jeffery's questions about it.

At the end of the cave I saw a faint light. I crawled over to it.

Perched on a small rock was a tiny jar topped with a cork piece. The jar was shiny glass and would probably fit into my palm perfectly. The jar contained yellow, floating, sparkly jelly-type stuff.

I grabbed the jar and found a tiny note tied around the top. I read it aloud to myself:

S is for sparkly.
S is for secrets.

S is for Spirit Horse.
S is for Snow.

"Snow!" I exclaimed.

It was her power! This yellow stuff, the stuff in the tiny jar, was Snow's life-saver. I tucked the jar into my pocket and dove back into the water, making sure I was clear of the rocks. Then I made my way to the water wall, crossed under it, and climbed out and onto a sandy bank.

"Yes!" I whispered to myself, staring at the tiny jar in my hand. This was *it!* I saved Snow!

I ran all the way back to Chayania. I didn't care if anybody saw me. I was too happy that Snow's power was finally found. I was even kind of happy that I was the one who found it.

"I found it!" I screeched as I jumped through a bush and into Chayania.

Alicia and Sasha were still there. Everyone looked at me with wide eyes.

I held out the jar and grinned.

Earth, Water, Alicia, and Sasha ran over to me.

"April! You aren't supposed to be here!" Alicia said.

"Why?" I said. "I just found Snow's power."

"Really?" Earth asked. She stared at the jar. "It is! That's it! That is Snow's power!"

"Told you," I said.

"Bring it here," Water said excitedly. She galloped back to Snow and waited as the rest of us walked over.

"Snow, you must drink this," Earth said, showing her the jar.

Snow could barely talk. "Give me."

I popped open the jar and tilted it into Snow's mouth. Snow gulped it down.

The next thing was beautiful. Snow stood. Her coat changed from almost-black to the whitest white a human could see. Her mane and tail grew long and snowy again, all traces of gray no where to be seen. Her eyes turned the same ice blue that they were when I met her. You could just see the strength coming back to Snow's body and eyes.

Everybody cheered for Snow as she grew to everyone else's sizes.

"Fire and Storm should be coming back soon," Water said. "They probably felt Snow's change."

I nodded. "Yeah. Change."

XIII

Change

ALICIA AND SASHA FOLLOWED ME out of Chayania.

"Congrats!" Sasha said, giving me a hug.

"On what?" I asked.

"You saved Snow's life!" Alicia replied.

"So you guys aren't mad?" I asked.

"No," Sasha said. "You saved a life."

"Snow isn't a life," I said. "She *was* a life, but now she's a spirit."

"Okay, then, you saved a spirit," Alicia said.

"I guess I did," I said, nodding.

"My mom's supposed to pick us up in fifteen minutes," Alicia said to Sasha.

"Oh, she doesn't have to," I said. "I can bring you guys home if you want."

"Okay," Sasha said.

Alicia called her mom and told her what was happening. Then we piled into my car and I drove out of the parking lot.

I stopped at the stop sign when Alicia asked, "What happened to your head?"

"Oh, it started bleeding when I was driving here," I told her.

"Oh," she replied.

Just as I drove out into the street after looking both ways, a screeching sound rang in my ears. I glanced around and finally spotted the tragic sighting ahead of me. A huge garbage truck was sliding toward Aunt Patty's tiny red car. I slammed on the brakes, but the man in the garbage truck's front seat didn't attempt to stop. We screamed.

This isn't like anything else. It isn't like when I got electrocuted by the fence in Brazil and I woke up a few hours later. It isn't like when I got hit by the rocks and I woke up in a safe place—home.

This time, I never wake up. Neither do my friends. This time, I'm like my parents—stuck, nowhere to run.

Life changes quickly. That's because there is no more life for you. It isn't your fault or anyone else's. You can't help it when you die—you can't choose when *not* to die. You can only choose when you do die.

But this was not one of those times.

Who wants to die? I didn't want to. I'm sure Alicia and Sasha didn't want to either. We were only sixteen. We were too young. Too young to get killed in a car accident. But at least we didn't have kids that had to deal with this. We had other family members, yes, but your own kid is just heart breaking.

Dying the same way my parents did isn't just weird. It's ironic. Because now I am going through the exact same thing that they did. I'll tell you, yes. I'll tell you that in a way I am still April Cincinnati. But I am also not April Cincinnati. I now have a new identity to proclaim and live up to.

Sand.

Heat.

Desert.